LEE PLETZERS

CHAOS

Chaos

Lee Pletzers

Seeing as how you just read all that small print tells us that you love words. So here are a few extra words just for you:

Syzygy /// Tmesis /// floccinaucinihilipilification

Author Note: This tale contains two creatures from the universe of H.P. Lovecraft. If you are unfamiliar with Lovecraft and his nightmarish creatures, please visit: http://en.wikipedia.org/wiki/Cthulhu _Mythos[2].

To save you time, the two creatures mentioned in this tale are:

Yog-Sothoth knows the gate. Yog-Sothoth is the key and guardian of the gate. Past, present, future, all are one in Yog-Sothoth — H. P. Lovecraft, "The Dunwich Horror"

(Reference Wikipedia)

Cxaxukluth (Androgynous Offspring of Azathoth) is one of the Seeds or Spawn of Azathoth, grown to adulthood and monstrous proportions and power.

(Reference Wikipedia)

(Author created cosmic entity.)

Zathuphu—a fictional cosmic entity described as a mix between a giant human, an octopus head, and the wings of a dragon. Zathuphu is described as able to change the shape of its body at will, extending and retracting limbs and tentacles.

In his house at Hivrla, dead Zathuphu waits to awaken and reclaim the world he once ruled.

For the lovers of Space Operas, Cyber Punk, and Science Fantasy

This book is dedicated to you.

Chaos

Screams filled the walkways. Lasers blasted. Something wet hit the wall and bounced off, landing with a thud in front of Laura and Jared Bester. They both stared down at the head of Interstellar Communications. Laura grabbed her brother's hand and they both ran. They dodged fighters carrying large weapons.

One passing fighter took Laura by the arm. "Get to the escape crafts," he shouted. "Hurry!"

An explosion not far from them took the fighter's attention.

Laura watched the fighter round the corridor. They heard a short shout and a thump in the corridor as the lower half of his body hit the wall and bounced onto the carpet. Something long and slimy like a snake, but black as night, slipped over the twitching legs, wrapped around them and, like a snapping rubber band, shot back around the corner and vanished.

Another explosion tore a chunk of metal from the wall.

The evacuation sirens screamed.

Chaos reigned.

Jared tugged on his sister's arm. "Escape crafts are this way."

Laura stared at the violence surrounding her. Part of her wanted to see the war, the battle, the creature that had invaded. Another part wanted to run, hide, and escape. A third part of her wanted to scream and crouch in the corner with her eyes closed.

"Laura!"

Jared's voice broke through to her and Laura nodded. "This way," she said.

They ran through corridors of smoke, fire, and screams. Red emergency lights flashed in rotating spheres. Laura lost her grip on Jared's hand. She grabbed him by the collar and led him through the madness and the ensuing terror.

Entering the evacuation chamber, they spotted seven solo-user escape pods and one solitary craft remaining. Laura's palm print opened the door; her studies in navigational mastery granted access to most shuttles for training purposes.

"Hurry up," she said, hustling Jared into the craft. He didn't seem to be paying attention, which was starting to frustrate her. She noticed his eyes focused on the door. "No one else is coming." In a gentle voice, she added, "We barely made it through ourselves."

Jared seemed to accept this and followed his sister into the control room. Two chairs faced the main viewer and Laura showed her brother how to lock in the safety harness. She did the same and then hit the automatic controls, sending them directly to Earth. Sending them back home.

The escape craft jerked as it broke free of the support structures. The loading bay doors opened and they were propelled out of a ship overrun by creatures that could scare her nightmares.

Thrusters engaged and the escape craft turned into a course for home. It brought the ship into view. Creatures had breached the hull. In the blackness of space, the fires leaping past ripped metal were especially bright.

Tears fell when the starship exploded.

The escape craft shuddered as the shockwave reached them. They were too close, but Laura had little control of the automatic navigator. The force was great and the judder became a jolt of power knocking the craft into a spin before a second shockwave slammed into the side sending it head-over-heels, flipping madly off course.

When momentum slowed Laura and Jared released the safety harness. No trace of the starship or its remains showed up in the viewer. She panned the view to all points of the compass.

She looked to Jared to see if he noticed the wrongness of their location. His confused expression showed he had also noticed the lack of stars and the lack of thruster power.

"Where are we?"

Laura kept panning the viewer. The automatic navigator on the control panel was nothing more than dead hardware. She tapped it with her fingers a few times to no avail.

"Laura?"

She had no answer for her brother.

LOST. FLOATING IN DARKNESS. Nothing anywhere. Silence their only friend. Jared sat in the co-pilot seat with his eyes shut. At barely thirteen, boredom came easy. Apart from the darkness, there was nothing to do or see. He checked the read-outs, hit the scan button, and waited for the same results that had returned for the past three months.

Nothing existed in that blackness out here, not even stars.

Jared leaned back in his seat and closed his eyes. He found it difficult to understand how he got into this with his sister. The events were blurry, everything was rushed and panic ran riot. They were being transported to Alpha-5 when his sister dragged him to an escape pod. He heard the shouting, the screams, the blood, smelled the fires raging. A one-month journey had turned into three months lost in space.

As a trainee navigator, Laura should know how to pilot this pod. But she couldn't; it contained a pre-programmed flight plan to take them back to Earth.

So what had happened? They both had no idea. One moment stars were beams of light stretching past, and then...darkness, complete and silent.

His sister entered the command center, her black hair hanging straight to her shoulders. She clipped him across the ears. "Wake up."

"I wasn't sleeping. I was thinking."

"Thinking. Really? About what?"

He spread his arms wide. "This."

"And what are your conclusions?"

"We're lost and the computer scans prove it. So much for pre-programmed."

Laura sat down in the commander's seat. "Maybe we didn't get far enough from the blast, which knocked out the guidance."

Jared shrugged. He didn't know anything about this stuff. He knew basketball and that had been enough, until now. "Your turn to keep watch."

"Whatever."

Jared exited. He waited for the door to whoosh shut behind him. That done, he went to his room. Escape pods weren't known for their roominess, so they were forced to share. One sonic shower, one eating quarters, and the command center. Designed for one month of transport.

In the sleeping quarters, he picked up his clothes off the floor. A sheet had been hung up separating the two beds. Privacy seemed important.

He opened the viewer screen. His eyes followed the panel as it slid into the wall. Darkness filled the view. Nothing new there. Jared hated space. It sucked. The pictures he'd seen at school and in books or holo-films made it look wonderful and beautiful. Lies, all of it.

Something smacked into the viewer.

Jared jolted back from the sound alone. The black sea of space stared back at him. He leaned closer, his nose almost on the glass. He could only see his reflection.

Cupping his hands against the glass, he stared out.

The thump against the glass repeated.

He ran to the sleeping quarters' entrance and waved his hand over the light panel. The darkness of the room matched that of the outside.

Jared's heart jackhammered against his chest. Slowly he moved in front of the viewer again.

Thud!

He saw it. It stuck to the glass this time—a vague shape against the viewer, barely an outline with eyes, a mouth, and teeth. It had five points like a starfish and each point had a mouth and tiny jagged teeth.

"Laura!" Jared bolted from the room. He dashed to the command center and slammed into the door he had shut. He waved his hand over the panel and the door slid open.

"What the hell are you doing?" Laura asked. She looked busy reading over the scanner. "Something's out there."

Jared tried to speak, but only panicked grunts came out.

Laura looked up. Seeing him, her face filled with alarm. She got off the chair. "Jared?" She grabbed him by the shoulders. "What's happened?"

He tried to answer but couldn't, so he pointed.

Laura looked down the hall. She could just see their room. She took a step forward, and Jared grabbed her arm and yanked back.

"No," he said. "No, no, no, no."

"It's all right. I'll be back in a minute."

Jared shook his head wildly.

"What am I looking for?" Laura asked.

"On...on...on th...th...the v...v...viewer."

"Inside or outside?"

Jared tried to calm his breathing. "Outside," he managed in one breath. His hands were twitching at his sides. Panic soared through his veins and he had to get it under control. He followed close behind Laura.

She waved her hand over the light panel, illuminating the room. She moved in front of the window. "I don't see anything."

Moving to the panel Jared plunged the room into darkness.

"Still nothing," she said.

"Just wait. I saw something, I swear."

They both stared outside, silence reigning over them. Jared's twitching stopped and his breathing returned to normal.

"I don't see anything," Laura whispered. "The scanners picked up something. It might have been space junk."

A loud *whoop, whoop, whooooop* sound filled the pod, ripping the air with urgency.

Laura bolted out of the room. Close on her heels, Jared followed into the control room. A red light flashed. She punched the light and a hologram appeared. Hovering just above the controls, she saw an image of a man's face. He looked at both of them.

"This is Commander Ryker of the AU Capricorn."

"The prison ship?" Laura asked.

"Correct. We are carrying seventy prisoners to Alpha-9. We spotted your distress signal."

Both Laura and Jared looked at each other. "We have a distress signal?"

"What is your situation?"

"We're lost," Jared said.

The commander smiled. "You're in dead space, son." He looked over his shoulder at someone off-screen. "Frankly, you're lucky we picked up your signal."

"Can you assist us? We're headed back to Earth," Laura said.

"We have to make a drop off first, then we will be heading back to New Australia." He looked down at his control panel. "Scanning your ship. One moment. Okay, here's the deal. We can transport you aboard but not the ship. You're too far to even tow. You have about three minutes to decide before the window closes."

"Yes," Jared and Laura said simultaneously.

"Good. Gather your essentials and be ready to transport in T minus two."

"We're ready now," Laura said.

Jared ran to the door. "Wait. I need my diary scan recorder." He bolted out the door before anyone could say anything. He ran into his room, leaving the lights off. He couldn't believe they had been found. Miracles did happen. They were in dead space; that answered many questions. There were no stars in dead space.

Nothing existed in such a place. Commander Ryker talked about a window. Did he mean a tunnel of some sort, a connecting thread through space? Pure luck. Excellent. He scooped up his diary off the floor and ran back to the control room, wrapping the flimsy black plastic around his wrist. "Ready," he said.

"Activating transport of three life forms."

"Three?"

The room turned pure white. Jared closed his eyes as the brightness grew, then it faded.

"Welcome aboard."

He opened his eyes to see a real bridge on a real starship. He counted ten people, all human, all wearing similar skin-tight jumpsuits, which were different only in their colors for positions and rank.

Commander Ryker wore green with three black V stripes on the chest. He looked muscular, like a bodybuilder. His chest, shoulders, and arms were bulked, pressing against his uniform. He had short black hair and a thin beard covered his cheeks. He stood in front of Jared.

"It's a lot to take in, isn't it?"

Jared nodded.

Ryker extended his hand. "And you would be...?"

"Jared." He shook the extended hand. "That's my sister, Laura."

Commander Ryker greeted her in the same way. "Welcome to the bridge," he said. "Where's the third member?"

"There's only the two of us," Laura said.

Ryker frowned. He looked past them. "Yuuma, you scanned three?"

Jared turned to see a thin Japanese man checking his controls. "Yes, sir. Three life forms."

"Damn it." He hurried to Yuuma's side and checked the scanner. "Then where's the third?" Checking his visitors, he said, "No cats or dogs?"

They both shook their heads.

Nodding, he said, "Demi, can you escort your two guests to spare quarters on the second level?"

"Aye aye, sir."

A woman with shoulder-length blond hair and wearing a blue jumpsuit approached them. "Come with me."

"And, guys, I'm going to need to know why you were aboard an escape craft. Have a rest first. At 1700, we can talk." Commander Ryker turned away from them.

As they exited, Jared asked Laura, "What's the time now?"

Laura shrugged.

"It's ten oh seven," Demi said, leading them from the bridge.

As they exited, they heard the commander order a full ship scan.

"Here you go." Demi opened the door. "Welcome to your new living space for the next six weeks. Hope you don't mind sharing."

"Thanks," Jared said. Laura seconded his appreciation.

"Okay, I'll give you a quick rundown."

Jared hadn't expected much but the room impressed him; spacious with sofas, an entertainment center, and one large bed. The sofas looked great. He decided he would sleep on one. Laura could have the bed. He had never slept on a sofa before. Lady Luck hung on his shoulder today.

Demi walked to a panel set in the wall. She pressed a button and a menu displayed to the right. "I think you will like our food selection." She pointed to a side door at the opposite end. "That's the sonic shower and the toilet is the door next to it." She looked at Jared and Laura in turn. "Would you like me to show you?"

"No thanks, Demi. I think we can handle it."

Jared studied the menu. "What's a hamburger?"

"Great food you won't find at home."

"Isn't that illegal?"

Demi smiled. "Not here. The Interstellar Council hasn't voted on it yet. When they do, Commander Ryker is going to cry."

This brought a smile from both.

"Indulge, guys. You both look starved." Demi waved her hand over the panel and the outer door opened. "If you need anything, just hit the comm panel." The door slid shut behind her.

"Why didn't you tell him?" Jared asked.

Laura looked confused. "Tell who what?"

"Commander Ryker, about the monster."

"Grow up. Nothing's out there."

"I saw it."

Laura shook her head. "You saw space junk."

"Then why were three life forms beamed on board?"

"It's a computer error, nothing more." Laura moved to get some food. "Space is empty," she said.

"I saw it. You didn't." Jared nodded as if he had just made an important decision. "I'm going to tell him." He moved to the door.

Laura flew across the room and blocked the exit panel activation. "Are you stupid?"

Jared said nothing.

"Do you want Commander Ryker to teleport us back to our escape vessel? He can if he thinks we're crazy."

"But I saw it."

Laura sighed. She put her arm around her brother and led him to the sofa. "You're my brother. You're also a pain in the butt. But I believe you saw something."

"It's a monster."

"You're a bit old for monsters, aren't you?"

Jared smiled. "Alien," he said.

"Space junk," Laura corrected.

"Whatever helps you sleep at night, sister." He jumped off the sofa before she could hit him. "I'm starved."

"Have a soon-to-be-illegal hamburger."

"Nah, I want healthy food."

Laura mocked a look of shock. "Oh my God, *you* are the alien. Give me back my brother." She smiled, showing a weak attempt at humor.

Jared smiled, but he couldn't find anything funny. He kept thinking about the third life form.

ROCK MODIFIED HIS CELL into a bodyweight training room. His mattress lay tossed against the bars. Only his cell had bars. All the other cells had electronic barriers, which gave an impression of space in the standard nine-by-four room.

Six high-tech prisons hadn't held Rock. With anything that relied on energy as a source of power, he could find a way out. Why the 'powers that be' thought he would want to break out of a heavily armed prison ship befuddled him. But things were as they were. He lived here, imprisoned in a cell from the early twentieth century while other cons had powered cells and access to holo-TV.

He had nothing. In the past three months, for amusement, Rock had started old-fashioned bodybuilding using his body weight as resistance. Every day he devised new routines that pushed him to maximize limited space and resources. His body slowly took on a shape that made him feel proud. He looked hard and mean, and he couldn't wait until they landed. No more cells and no more prison guards. Prisoners forging for themselves, a new start in an old-style way of life.

And on the plus side, there would be women, prisoners, as well.

The downside meant no communication off-world, no electricity, and no drugs. Yep, there always is a harsh downside.

Rock finished a series of pushups, stood, and stretched. He flexed his chest for that little extra blood flow, then relaxed. He rolled his shoulders and kicked the mattress up hard against the bars. On the floor with his legs bent, he wriggled under the bed and gripped the frame to perform a series of pull-ups.

Something shot past his head.

Probably just a cockroach, he thought. All types of vermin entered his cell. Electronic barriers on other cells zapped them dead. Another downside. On the plus side, if there were two, he could race them. The thought brought a smile to his face—a face that hadn't done a lot of smiling in the past. Getting old and getting soft. He didn't like that. At close to fifty, he still looked thirty and now had the body to match that age. His excitement at landing in the new world with women looking for hard, tough men brought visions of a life he had never considered before. A plan formed in his mind when he'd learned of the off-world transfer. A new life. A new start. Perhaps a new man would emerge as well.

Something bumped his head.

"Son of—" He released the frame and turned onto his stomach. The sight that greeted him stopped his words. It looked like a starfish, but the points were used as legs. It glared at him with eyes so small, Rock could barely see them.

That ain't no cockroach.

The creature shimmered and then latched onto his face faster than a spider's jump. He didn't see it move. The points it used for legs stuck into his face. He felt small teeth biting, digging through his flesh. He wanted to scream but its body covered his mouth. Something slimy inserted up his nose and kept going. He felt pressure behind his forehead. A sudden jolt of intense pain seared into the bone and he almost passed out. Subsiding as quickly as it had started, the pain faded.

The being dropped off his face and its points folded into itself like a spider dying.

Rock felt his face. His fingers came away covered in blood, but that didn't bother him. Gently prodding his nose, he could feel something lodged in there and instinctively knew it had attached to his brain. Somehow, he also knew that the starfish thing had been only a carrier, a shell for transport, and nothing more.

He turned his palms up and saw a tiny hole in each hand. The skin cracked and the hole stretched. Small white teeth formed. He brought his hands to his face and whispered, "Ph'nglui mglw'nafh Zathuphu R'lyeh wagh'nagl fhtagn." He had no idea what he had said and yet somehow, he understood the meaning. He whispered, "Soon he will awake."

Black filled his vision and he passed out.

JARED ATE HIS FILL until he could eat no more. Having been hungry for such a long time, he eyed the food only seconds before eating it with gusto. Laura ate at a slow, reserved pace, but Jared didn't care. Starvation had taken control. He could have eaten a horse if such creatures existed outside of school holo-texts. Still, he didn't eat the hamburger. He had no idea how his body would react to that food.

Full and sleepy and happy—three of his new favorite things. He lay on the sofa and pulled the diary off his wrist, stretched it across his head, and thought of all that had happened in the past few days. He omitted the thing he saw stuck on the viewer of the escape pod. He also omitted the third life form beamed onboard.

With the diary updated, he closed his eyes and waited for sleep. His eyes were closing, blurring out the features of their new quarters.

He repositioned himself on the sofa when something hit him.

Opening his eyes, he sat up. Laura had thrown the holo-scan at him. "What?"

"You're a little creep."

Jared stared at his sister, shocked. What had brought this on? Had he done something unknowingly in his one minute of sleep? Hundreds of questions flew through his mind, but he managed to say only one word: "What?"

Laura got off the bed. She looked taller and more muscular than before. "This is all because of you."

"I'm sorry." Jared had no idea why he felt the need to apologize and it didn't seem to calm down his enraged sister. "What did I do?"

A low rumbling growl came from deep in his sister's throat.

Jared straightened up on the sofa, drawing his knees to his chest. He wanted to run, but his body refused his commands. Paralyzed, he sat there and stared at his sister.

She seemed to grow in height as the growl in her throat deepened and her top lip curled up like a dog on edge. Less than a foot from him, Laura slowly raised her arms until she looked like the letter Y.

Laura threw her head back and took a deep breath. Slowly lowering her head, Jared saw tentacles withering from her cheeks, snaking left and right in an uncontrolled frenzy, as they tried to find something to grab hold. Opening her mouth revealed a cluster of jagged yellow teeth.

"Wgah'nagl Zathuphu azathoth nog n'ghft gof'nn shugg." Laura leaned forward, almost nose to nose with Jared.

He wanted to sink into the sofa and disappear but couldn't. His sister whispered the words again. Each word produced a picture in his head, not a translation like foreign languages.

Wgah'nagl (house of) *Zathuphu* (high priest) *azathoth* (child of chaos) *nog* (brings) *n'ghft* (darkness) *gof'nn* (children) *shugg* (Earth).

"The house of Zathuphu, a child of chaos, brings darkness to the children of Earth," Jared whispered.

Laura smiled. Her teeth were terrifyingly close to his face. Lightning fast, she latched onto Jared. He screamed, kicking and thrashing.

"Jared, stop it. Wake up." Laura held him in a tight hug. "Wake up. Wake up."

The words seeped into Jared through the haziness of the nightmare. He stopped kicking. His chest heaved up and down, his heart raced, but as the room came into focus and Laura's smiling face looked upon him with a hint of concern, it slowed quickly. He pulled free of his sister's grip and stared at her wide-eyed.

"Say those words," he said.

"Wake up, wake up."

"Not them. The weird language."

"I have no idea what you are talking about." She ruffled his hair. "You were screaming like a little girl."

"Was not."

"Was too." Laura got off the sofa. "You've been out for an hour."

Jared sat up on the sofa. "I had a weird dream. You were speaking in strange words and I understood them."

"Uh-huh," Laura said, her attention turned to the food and drink machines menu. "Wanna drink? They have heaps of juices here. Perfect for a little girl."

"Ha ha," he replied, not having a decent comeback. "You had a mouthful of yellow teeth."

"All the better to eat you with, my dear." Laura approached the sofa carrying two tall glasses of green grass juice. She handed one to Jared who gulped his down.

Jared lay back down on the sofa for lack of anywhere else to go.

"I'm going to explore," Laura said, taking the glasses to the recycling unit.

"I want to come with."

"Fine, but I'm going now." She headed for the door.

Jared scrambled off the sofa and rushed through the door. He found his sister reading a map. He took a look himself, amazed at the size of the ship. There were several levels. The first three levels acted as quarters for staff. One section down contained maintenance staff and their quarters. The next five floors were colored in red and labeled *Transport*. The next level took up a large section of the map, easily the size of a three-story house, and read *Engine Room*. Each level had two accesses, by *elevator* or *Steps*. In the Red Zone, two areas were marked *Guards' Quarters*.

"They have a transport room," Jared said. "Can't they just teleport us back?"

"Don't be daft. It's too far. We'd get scrambled and arrive home inside out if we even make it back. It's too risky, otherwise, Commander Ryker would have done that straight away."

Jared nodded. It made sense.

"Besides, I don't think 'Transport' means teleportation."

"What is it then?"

"This is a prisoner ship, remember?"

"Oh, yeah."

A door at the far end of the corridor opened and Demi came out with a smile on her face. "Exploring, are we?"

Both Laura and Jared nodded.

"It can get boring out here with nothing to do."

"What does 'Transport' mean?" Jared asked.

"It's the prison section of the ship," Demi said. Her voice turned serious, "Don't go down there, ever. Do you both understand that?"

They nodded.

"Do you like games?" Demi asked, looking at Jared.

"Yes, ma'am," he replied.

"Good. I happen to have a holo console that you can borrow. It's old and the neuro-emotions connector doesn't work well." She smiled and said, "But it has a zombie game, Western shoot 'em up, and a few space wars you might enjoy."

Jared beamed.

"And for you, young lady," Demi's smile continued, "do you know what my position is here?"

Laura shook her head.

"I'm second navigational officer. Your file came up as 'in training' on the system. How about resuming training while you're stuck here? You'll be near fully qualified when you get back home."

Laura smiled.

ROCK GOT UP OFF THE floor, dazed and slightly confused. What had just happened? He performed a self-pat-down, checking for injuries. A steel plate welded to the wall served as his mirror. A trickle of blood flowed from his nose.

"We are here to bring the great one," he said, surprised at the sound of his voice. "We are now one." He looked at his reflection. Rock couldn't be sure but he swore his lips hadn't moved that time.

He shut his eyes and took a deep breath to calm down. He feared his mind had finally broken. After years of violence and hate, his fragile mind had snapped.

The image of a starfish appeared against his eyelids—a vicious creature that appeared benign. He suddenly remembered what happened and barely made it to the toilet bowl as a rush of vomit spewed forth.

With closed eyes, he dropped to his knees and hugged the cold metal. A second belt took flight without warning and he heard lumps hit the small pool of water. Ready to flush the gunk away, he checked. Expecting to see small chunks of carrot, instead, he gazed upon a sludge of black goo sliding down to the water.

"What the hell?"

A third cramp hit his stomach. A moment later, more bile surged up his throat, making a loud *plonk* as it hit. One solid lump. Looking at it and breathing hard, it took a moment to realize his small nosebleed had become a major nnosebleed

Whispered words he neither knew nor understood filled his head. The words sounded like jumbled phonics and gibberish. But within moments, they formed a rhythmic pulse beating in time with the drops of blood bouncing off the sludge. He turned his hands palm up and saw the small hole in each. They were slits—closed mouths waiting for the chance to sink teeth into flesh.

Rock staggered to his feet. He lost his balance twice and dropped onto the metal frame of his bed. Uneasily getting to his feet, he made his way to the bars. Balance became difficult on two legs; he preferred four or eight. That made walking easier. He swayed back and forth, holding onto the bars. Words would not be a problem—access to vocabulary was automatic—but first, he had to steady this body.

Practicing his balance, Rock walked from one end of the cell to the other and back. He did this several times until the steps became smooth and effortless.

Back at the bars, he screamed, "Guard. Quick!"

A speaker overhead crackled to life. "What is it?"

He had expected a guard to show up. He had not thought to access memories. Now he did, searching for a reason to get a guard to open the cell door.

"What is it?" the voice repeated.

Thinking fast, Rock said, "I want to speak with my son one last time before we land."

A reply took a long time in coming. "You refused to speak to Sam the last time he called."

"I just now realized the mistake. It's my last opportunity. Plus, in the toilet is some black slime I puked up. That can't be good."

"Stand back from the bars."

Rock did as ordered.

A minute later, a chubby man in an ill-fitting silver suit without a tie appeared. He had short-cropped hair and gray, day-old stubble covering his round cheeks. The man studied

Rock, looking him up and down before saying, "What's this I hear about you wanting to speak to Sam?"

"Warden Johnson. What a surprise."

The warden stared at him with cold, hard eyes.

Rock wished the warden would move just two steps closer to the cell bars. "I've had an emphatic realization."

"I never took you for the sentimental type."

"Because I always thought I had time to right wrongs. Now I don't."

The warden's voice softened. "I can understand that. Do you think Sam will want to talk to you?"

Rock pretended to think this over. Slowly he nodded, then shrugged his shoulders. "I'm hoping so."

The warden smiled. "Then let's give it a shot. We can only but try."

Rock took another step away from the bars to show he posed no threat and had zero intention of trying anything.

Nodding, the warden turned to face the operators and the other guards. "Bring out the shackles. Old style, not electronic." He turned back to Rock. "I see you have kept up the training," he said, motioning to the mattress on the floor. The smile dropped from his face. "What's that?"

"What?"

"Under the bed frame."

Rock bent to look and saw the dead starfish. It resembled a normal sea creature now.

"Step away!" Warden Johnson had a strong and authoritative voice. He had his phaser pointed in Rock's direction. "Now!"

Doing as told, Rock said, "It just appeared out of thin air."

To someone out of Rock's view, Warden Johnson said, "Call a sweeper and get Commander Ryker on the comms."

The guard arrived and passed iron shackles through the bars to Rock. Worried that the discovery of the starfish had ruined his chances of getting his hands on a guard or the warden, he put the heavy latches around his ankles, then his wrists.

"Warden, Commander Ryker is coming down."

"Very well, get the sweeper on stand-by and take this prisoner to a holo-communicator."

"Yes, sir," Guard Patterson said. He turned to face the cell. "Turn around and back up to the bars with your hands as far behind you as possible."

Rock complied and felt his shackles tightened and padlocked across his back. Then he heard the cell door clank open and allowed himself to be pulled from the cell backwards with Guard Patterson holding firmly to the shackles.

Rock stared at the warden as he passed rows of silent or hushed cells. Everyone watched him. He stole a few glances in their directions and all but one quickly looked down at their feet. They knew him—knew the depths of darkness he would go to for his needs, desires and wants. Rock was not one to mess about.

"Your reputation precedes you," Warden Johnson said.

"Perhaps they want me to free them?"

"You'll all be free soon enough."

They reached the end of the cell block.

"Warden, sir, Commander Ryker is here. He is waiting outside your office."

Warden Johnson nodded. "Get the thing bagged and brought to my office immediately."

"Yes, sir."

Rock's palms were itchy. "Soon," he whispered.

"You say something, prisoner?"

"Not a word, guard."

"That's Guard Patterson to you, prisoner."

"Who names their son Guard?"

"Your mama."

Rock laughed. "Nice retort," he said.

Someone pulled him from behind. "Keep moving or that phone call expires."

"Yes, Guard Patterson."

ON HER WAY TO THE BRIDGE to continue her training, Laura couldn't believe her luck. Concern niggled at the back of her mind about getting into the program once she returned home.

Demi opened the doors with her DNA print scan and bade her to enter. There were two seats near the front of the bridge and two control panels behind them. Against the curved wall were a myriad of controls from the engine room to the prison cells, to workers' quarters and general operations of the ship, and...navigation. Two rotating seats were positioned in front of two identical panels.

"I'll log you in to semi-B navigational. You'll be able to practice on that. Follow the read-outs and tell me where we are going."

"Yes, ma'am." Laura took her seat and looked around at a real bridge, not a holo-projection that she had studied with previously. "Where's Commander Ryker?"

A young man stepped up to her. "He's dealing with the third life form."

"A third?" *Jared was right?*

"Yes, ma'am, but it is lifeless."

"If it is lifeless, how did the scanners pick it up?"

"Many questions," he said, a smile planted on his face. "The scanners detect organic matter with a distinct DNA sequence and classify it as a life form. It arrived dead or died on arrival. The teleport came from Dead Space via radio waves, so unfortunately we can't be certain."

Demi broke into their conversation. "Laura, let me introduce Ensign Coffey."

"Pleased to meet you." He extended his hand.

"Hi, I'm Laura."

He smiled again. "I know."

Demi said, "You're logged in."

"Thank you."

"So, first, tell me what you know."

PUSHED INTO A SMALL room consisting of a chair and a video phone, Guard Patterson unhooked the arm restraints on Rock so he could operate the phone. The small room could fit three people and no more. Behind them, the barrier door shut. Placing his palm on the scanner, Rock spoke his name.

"DNA read-out not recognized," a computerized voice said from the phone screen.

"Try again," Guard Patterson said in a tired voice. "It's not the most updated phone."

"Something's wrong with my palm," Rock said.

"Nah, it's just the phone is old. It's a video phone for crying out loud. It's the only off-world phone that still works regardless of new technology." Patterson sighed. "It's a piece of junk."

"Sometimes old works better."

"It does in your case with your cell. You ain't going anywhere."

Rock rubbed his palms together. "They hurt."

Guard Patterson stepped closer and grabbed Rock's hands. "Nothing there, sissy."

Smiling, Rock said, "Watch."

The palms split open.

"What the hell?" A mouth formed on both palms. Guard Patterson stumbled back, but Rock grabbed him around the throat with one hand. Tiny teeth started chewing. A scream, choked by fear, eked out before the other hand clamped over the guard's mouth. A small, thin, snakelike appendage, with tiny black dots for eyes, exited the mouth and slid across Guard Patterson's cheek, searching for the nose.

Removing his hand from the now blood-gorged mouth, Rock flexed his fingers and gently prodded it in the right direction. Blood rolled over Patterson's chin and dribbled to the floor.

The alien slid into Patterson's nose. A moment later, the man dropped. Before he hit the floor, Rock caught and held him upright. "You can't fight it," he said. "This human tried and failed, as you will fail as well."

Patterson shut his eyes. When he reopened them, they were dull, lifeless orbs. He smiled.

Rock went to the barrier. "Hey!" he shouted. "Patterson's hurt."

An unknown guard opened the barrier and rushed to help. A few seconds later, he too had an alien life force pushing into his brain and taking control.

"Patterson," Rock said, "open the cells and make all like us." To the unknown guard, he said, "Who are you?"

"We are one."

"Yes, we are one. What is your human name?"

"John Smith."

"Okay, John Smith, you go to the guards' quarters and do the same. When we are all together, I will summon the great Priest, Zathuphu, and as one we shall return to Earth and inherit all that we lost an age ago."

"There are two hundred prisoners on two levels. This will take time."

Nodding, Rock considered his choices. "Smith, after you have dealt with the guards, go with Patterson and help him. I will talk with Commander Ryker and the warden. We will gather here in three hours. Is that enough time, Patterson?"

Patterson nodded.

"Then get to it. And remember, no one touches the warden or Ryker but me." Rock turned away from them.

As he exited the phone room, he heard shouts from further down the hall. That had to be Smith. Rock didn't worry about the noise. Once the human Smith lost the battle for his consciousness, things would move smoothly and fast.

Soon Zathuphu would awake and the Elder gods would join him. Together they would rape the Earth and quash the mortals. Both the magic of the old days and The Watcher would exist no more. Nothing could stop them. He felt a smile spread across his face as he reached the warden's office.

LAURA HAD SPENT THE last hour learning how the navigational panel worked. It looked similar to the training board at school.

"Let's take a break," Demi said. "I have some logs to fill before the next shift."

"Okay." Laura didn't need or want a break, but she had no intention of speaking out.

"We'll continue in ten hours." Demi stood up.

"Shall I log off?"

Demi reached over and tapped a few light numbers. "All done." She started looking for something. "Wait here."

Watching her leave, Laura wished she had brought her textbooks like Jared had brought his diary. The thought hadn't crossed her mind during the rescue.

"Hi there."

She turned to see Ensign Coffey standing next to her. A lump suddenly formed in her throat and her pulse increased.

"I hope Demi isn't driving you too hard," he said as Demi returned.

In her hand she carried a thin, rectangular metal bar. She gave it to Laura. "Homework," she said. "Swipe your hand across the surface and a star map will appear. Plot a course to the nearest sun."

"Sure thing. Thanks."

"I'm off duty now. May I escort you to your quarters?"

Laura looked at Ensign Coffey and then at Demi, who smiled. "Thank you," she said, getting off her chair. Together they exited the bridge.

An uncomfortable silence followed them to the lifts. Ensign Coffey pressed the button and waited. His hands twitched at his sides.

Laura decided to break the silence. "So, how long have you been an ensign?"

"This is my third year and my fifth journey."

"I see. Why?"

"When were you last back home?"

Laura smiled. "A very long time ago."

"Well, ever since New Zealand and Australia merged—officially—work has been kind of scarce. Genetic farms take only scientists looking for new ways to produce food following ANZAC guidelines, and according to my brainwave report, I'm not suited to office work. I could either be an ensign or some form of government employee."

"Do you prefer off-world life?"

"It has its moments. And we have an excellent holo-cinema."

"I haven't seen a movie in years."

"Well, if you have time, I can take you."

"I want to, but I need to speak with Commander Ryker at 1700 hours."

Ensign Coffey looked at his bare wrist and blue digits appeared. "Eighty minutes away."

The lift doors opened and they stepped in at the same time.

"Living Quarters L2, please."

"So, that's my address," Laura said. She couldn't help herself from smiling.

"It is indeed."

Laura gave him a strange look.

"I'm sorry," he said. "We don't meet many people way out here. I'm not used to talking with people, apart from following commands and offering reports." He shrugged.

"How old are you, Ensign?"

"Nineteen. You?"

"Sixteen. My brother is thirteen."

"Oh, yes. How is your brother adjusting?"

The lift doors opened.

"Let's go see," she said.

WARDEN JOHNSON MET Commander Ryker outside his office. "I apologize for holding you up, Commander."

"Not a problem, Warden. You have a busy job."

"Rock wanted to reconcile with his son." The warden shook his head. "A bit late for that, I feel. But we must give the man a chance." He pulled out a chair in front of his desk and offered it to Commander Ryker, who took the seat without a word. The warden sat in his seat behind his desk.

"What can I do for you?" Commander Ryker asked.

The intercom buzzed.

"Yes?"

"Warden, the sweepers have the item bagged."

"Very good. Commander Ryker is in my office. Bring it here."

"Yes, sir."

"What is it?" Commander Ryker asked, leaning forward in his seat.

The warden's eyebrows rose. "Are you looking for something?" Johnson had never seen the Commander so interested in anything brought to his attention before.

"The grapevine moves fast, even out in space."

"I noticed the scan."

"You shouldn't have."

"It came up on my screen."

"What is it?"

The warden clasped his hands under his chin. "I'd love to know how it got on board."

Commander Ryker narrowed his eyes. He stared hard at the warden, made a decision and relaxed, leaning back in his seat. "I'm the law out here," he said.

"I'm aware of that. You have the full cooperation of my men and myself."

Commander Ryker nodded. "We came across a distress signal. Two human children. We beamed them onboard. Unfortunately, something else came with them."

"Something did." A knock came at the door. A halo-image of an officer the warden didn't know appeared in the door. He waved his hand over the green open light next to the drawer of his desk. "This is the item we discovered in a prisoner's cell."

The officer brought in a small white box and placed it on the warden's desk.

"We discovered it quite by accident. As mentioned earlier, we released Rock to make a call to his son and that's when it was spotted." The warden reached for the box.

Commander Ryker held out his hand. "Wait." He sat forward in his seat.

"It's dead."

"We can't be sure of that."

"It's a starfish, Commander. There's none in our oceans anymore, but apparently one got into space somehow." He opened the box, looked in, and then held it out to the commander.

The commander seemed apprehensive at first to take it.

Warden Johnson poked the item inside. "Very dead, sir."

Commander Ryker smiled. "You can never be too careful. Space has a way of making the innocent dangerous."

The warden stopped poking.

Ryker took it and looked inside. "It's a starfish," he stated. From his jumpsuit, he removed a medic scanner and ran the bright beam of white light across the surface, reading its vitals and genetic makeup. The tiny holographic light on the scanner produced the information in a V-shaped beam of light. Ryker read it. "It's completely dead. Harmless now." Pressing a side button on the scanner, he forwarded the details to the ship's physician, closed the box, and handed it back to the warden. "Have this sent to the good doctor, will you?"

"Aye aye, sir."

Commander Ryker stood. "And tell no one of this." He turned toward the door. "This incident doesn't go in your report, it doesn't get logged and it doesn't go past this section. Do you understand?"

The warden nodded.

"Good."

The door opened. The warden stared at it. He hadn't operated the door. How could this be possible, and what the hell was Rock doing standing in the doorway?

"Commander Ryker," Rock said. "It's a pleasure to finally meet you."

Ryker stared at the man. "And you would be?"

"The first of seven," Rock said. His hand shot out covering Commander Ryker's mouth and his other hand clasped the back of his neck, pinching a spinal nerve, holding him motionless.

Pain twisted Ryker's face.

Warden Johnson radioed for security. He watched helplessly as a snake-like form emerged from Rock's hand and wriggled up into the commander's nose.

Rock released Commander Ryker.

The commander removed his phaser and aimed at Rock. Rock smiled. The phaser dropped from Ryker's hand as several security guards entered the warden's office.

"Grab him," Warden Johnson ordered.

The security guards rushed around the desk to the warden and grabbed him by the arms and around his head. They pushed him against the wall, holding him firmly in place.

Commander Ryker dropped to the floor. His hands clawed at his face.

"Don't fight it," Rock said. "Your death will be less painful." He walked over to the warden. "You seriously thought I'd come here without backup already established?"

John Smith stumbled through the door and fell to his knees next to Commander Ryker. He quickly got to his feet. Blood oozed from his nose.

Rock moved around the desk. "Three of Seven, what happened?"

He wiped at his nose. "I don't know. I just started bleeding. I'm losing the grip."

"You were meant to kill the soul."

"Couldn't find it."

The warden laughed. "Pathetic," he said. "Souls don't exist. All religion was debunked years ago."

Rock stormed over to Warden Johnson. His arm rose, exposing the mouth with jagged teeth. He slammed his hand against the warden's mouth. "You don't need to believe to have one."

The warden struggled as he saw the snakelike thing slither toward his nose.

John Smith started screaming incoherent words. He gripped his head and staggered around the room. He spied something on the floor, bent down quickly, and picked up Commander Ryker's phaser. The screaming stopped.

Rock turned, removing his hand. The alien scurried into the warden's nose. The phaser was aimed at him. "What are you doing, John?" He used the man's real name.

Tears of blood ran down John's eyes.

Rock moved forward a step.

John closed his eyes and then opened them again. "I can't hold him for long. I wanted to serve you. Goodbye." He placed the phaser against his head and fired. Blood and meat splattered against the opposite wall and dribbled down in small trails. He hit the floor as Commander Ryker stood up.

"Welcome, Commander Ryker. You just got promoted to Three of Seven."

Ryker nodded. "Soul destroyed."

"Good."

"Mine too," Warden Johnston added.

Rock smiled. There were now Four of Seven. As the original, Rock knew he had to covert three more to make the seven. All the inmates that the others like Patterson converted would be the second and third or fourth generation. They would not do, regardless of how many hundreds existed.

"Three more," he whispered. *Then I would have the Seven of Seven for the calling of Zathuphu.* And the girl, he noticed on the escape craft, would be the great priest's vessel.

LAURA WAVED HER HAND to open the door. Both she and Ensign Coffey entered. A soft blue light encased Jared. Sweat beaded his face and he held both hands out in front, in a grip, as if holding a weapon of some sort. He spun around and swore using chic words from the twentieth century.

Engrossed in the virtual reality game, he had no idea they were there. He couldn't see or hear them. The only images he saw and sounds he heard were from the game—an outlawed game that had a tendency to blend reality with the game if the player partook too much.

She didn't mind Jared playing the game, but there had to be a time limit. She walked over to the console and switched the imager off.

Jared kept firing a few more times before realizing the game had ended. He looked confused for a few moments longer until Laura stepped into his line of sight. "You've played enough for one day."

"Oh, come on, it's only been an hour."

"Did you start when I left with Demi?"

Jared nodded.

Laura raised her eyebrows.

"Oh," he said, disappointed. "That's a good game. I've never played anything like it."

"Enjoy it while it lasts, buddy," Coffey said.

Jared looked at him, and then at Laura. "Who's that?"

"This is Ensign Coffey. He's a friend," Laura said.

"Already?"

She slapped him across the head. "Ignore my socially challenged brother," she said to Ensign Coffey.

"No worries. He'll fit in well here." He smiled at Jared who didn't return the gesture.

"I'm hungry," Jared said.

"You know where the food dispenser is," Laura said. "We're meeting Commander Ryker soon, so eat now."

"Yes, Mum."

"I'd better be getting a move on," Ensign Coffey said.

Laura approached him. "Why not join us for an early dinner, or a coffee or something?"

"Or something," Jared said, deftly dodging his sister's swinging hand and laughing as he ran to the food dispenser. He looked at the menu. "Can I try a hamburger?"

"I thought you wanted healthy food."

Jared shrugged. "This is the only time I can try one."

"Go ahead," she said. Laura knew she should have said no, but what would one hurt and it did contain vegetables. She turned her attention back of Ensign Coffee. "Sorry about that."

"No worries."

"Just a coffee?" Laura asked.

"There's always tomorrow," Coffey said. "Oh eight hundred, breakfast?"

"Aye aye, Ensign Coffey." Laura saluted him.

He didn't return it but laughed as he exited the room.

Turning to her brother, she said, "I want you to set a timer on that game. One hour, then a two-hour break for reading or doing something else. Those things were banned back home. Maybe you remember that?"

"Yeah, but I'd never played one before." Jared carried his hamburger to the table. "It's really awesome, Laura. You should try it."

"Zombie Killer. No, thanks."

"Can I play after dinner?"

"No more tonight."

"Oh, please?"

"No. I don't want you going crazy."

"I won't."

"Can't take that chance. You're already pretty whacko," she said with a smile. At the food dispenser, she ordered a salad. Together they ate in silence, enjoying their food. Laura looked over at Jared. He was ripping into his hamburger. She knew he would miss that once they got back to Earth.

Would I miss Ensign Coffey?

Fork almost to her mouth, she stopped eating. Where the hell had that thought come from? She had just met him. He seemed like a nice enough guy, but she would have to be crazy to wonder if she'd miss him. Yet none of the boys she had dated before brought such feelings, this quickly. Never a love-sick puppy, she neither believed in nor read romance books. Laura had her feet solidly on the ground and knew where she wanted to go in life and what she wanted to achieve. Besides, Ensign Coffey was older than her. He probably didn't see her as anything more than someone to entertain while stranded on a prison ship.

"Aren't you eating?" Jared asked.

Laura looked at her food. "Guess not," she said.

"Are you thinking about that beverage guy?"

"Shut up."

Jared finished his dinner, licked his fingers, and yawned. "Think I'll take a sonic shower and go to bed early." He rose slowly from the sofa and returned his plate to the dispenser, stretched, and headed for the shower. "I'm more tired than I thought."

"Don't forget Commander Ryker's interviewing us at 1700." She looked at the clock it was 1810 now. He was running late. She would wait a few hours and if he showed up, she could wake Jared. Exhausted, she hoped she could also stay awake.

Not answering, Jared headed into the shower room. "No way!"

"What's wrong?"

"They have actual water."

Laura couldn't believe her ears. She rushed into the shower room just as Jared removed his trousers.

"Hey!"

She backed out of the room, covering her eyes. "I'm blind! I'm blind!"

The door slid shut behind her.

A real water shower. It blew her mind. She knew ocean water was filtered into drinking water but not showers. Things sure had changed on Earth. She couldn't wait to get back. Maybe the air was clean as well...

ROCK EXITED THE WARDEN'S office with Commander Ryker and Warden Johnston close on his heels. A couple of convicts who hadn't been converted ran past them. It didn't matter how far they got, they would soon serve real gods.

They reached the elevator as Patterson caught up to them. "Most are converted, Rock. Some died, a few escaped and the rest are awaiting orders."

The elevator doors swished open.

Rock said, "Distribute the men in groups of three and go floor by floor converting everyone. There's a few hundred on board."

"Actually, there is one thousand and seventeen, including Bridge and secondary facilities."

"Even better," Rock said. "This task may take a few hours. Meet us at the Bridge when you're finished."

"Aye aye, sir." Patterson ran off looking eager to please.

"Take us to the Bridge, Commander."

Ryker pressed his thumb against the panel and the elevator doors closed.

They rode in silence until the doors opened on the Bridge. Commander Ryker strode out. There were only a few workers on the evening shift. Two stood near Navigation and were in a soft conversation, three sat at their stations, and one played on a tablet. Three others were seated in a circle away from their stations. No one noticed his unexpected arrival; the commander never came up during the evening shift.

Rock stood back letting the commander take the lead.

Someone noticed them and shouted, "Officer on deck!" Instantly everyone snapped to attention. Those not near their workstations looked guilty, knowing they should never be away from their posts.

"Relax, everybody." Commander Ryker walked up to the vacant navigation station.

The two workers standing near it quickly took their seats, and waved their hands over the panels, lighting them. The young officer closest to Ryker said, "All systems are good, sir, and we are on track to dispatch the prisoners within the allotted time frame." He looked up at Rock, recognizing him instantly and confusion clouded his features.

"My, I am famous, aren't I?" Rock said, stepping forward. "Commander, if you wouldn't mind..." He motioned to the young officer. Ryker raised his hand. The officer tried to get out of the way, but the officer next to him blocked his path. Ryker's hand slammed into the guy's face, his palm covering the mouth and nose.

A female officer ran up to the commander, requesting him to stop, but Warden Johnson grabbed her face in the same manner. The creature slid out of his palm and wriggled up her nose. The woman dropped to the floor next to the officer Ryker had converted. Both twitched and then lay still.

A man made a move to the alarm system but Rock quickly blocked him, grabbed him around the neck, and hoisted him up. "What do you think you are doing?" His voice stayed calm, which made it all the more ominous. He tossed him like a sack of potatoes to the floor at Johnson's feet.

The warden needed no prompting and quickly put his hand to work.

Ten minutes later, everyone, bar the two dead, was ready to follow Rock's bidding. He had thought they would come around as the commander had, but not all vessels were strong enough to handle the conversion.

"Commander, re-program our course. We're going home to Earth."

"Computer, enter new course bearings for New Australia."

A computerized voice said: "*Unable to follow command. Course program is locked.*"

Ryker tried again but got the same response. He ran his hands through his hair, then tapped several light buttons.

"*Enter password.*"

"Password?" he wondered aloud. "Override is meant to override all systems and security." After several attempts, he looked at Rock for orders.

Rock asked everyone, "Does anyone know the override password?"

One female officer slowly and sheepishly raised her hand. "Tony did," she said, pointing to the dead officer on the floor.

"Who else?"

"Demi," Commander Ryker said. "She's head of navigation."

"Warden, go fetch her, will you? Don't turn her yet."

Johnson stopped at a side panel, typed in his access code, and located her quarters. "Got it," he said. Rock had chosen well to have the warden on his side; his access codes could open as many doors as Commander Ryker's.

Taking a stroll around the Bridge, Rock was impressed by the layout. Everything seemed to be in a perfect location, both aesthetically and functionally. This was a higher-level craft than the previous boat he had been on. He stopped at the front. "How do I see outside?"

Commander Ryker sat in his chair. "Viewer up," he commanded, and the front of the Bridge turned black, then white lights of varying sizes came into view.

Rock studied the stars. He looked from left to right to left again. In his head, he saw a star map and tried to locate his position in the black void. There was nothing to indicate his position and he remembered they had yet to turn.

What was taking the warden so long?

He wasn't worried about time. There were sixteen hours left before he really had to start to worry. The last time they had been this close to success, a few of the older gods were in transition, partially through the doorway he had created, then some sneaky filthy human—

"Commander Ryker," he said.

The commander looked up.

"Disable the self-destruct program."

Ryker scratched his chin. "I'll try, but I think that's a built-in hardware issue." A screen appeared in front of him. He tapped commands and studied the screen before nodding. "I can remove the access to the software that starts the destruct countdown, but to remove it, someone has to physically disengage the explosives on the first three floors and the last two floors." He looked at Rock, his face devoid of emotion. "It can also be started from any one of these points manually. One explosion will flick the switch on the computer's AI and it will initiate a section-by-section detonation."

Rock pointed at three officers. "You heard him. Manually disable the bombs and stay put. You are ordered to guard the locations and never leave your new post until we land back home."

The three gave a curt nod and headed to the door.

As they stepped out, Demi entered with the warden gripping her arm. A cut leaked blood over her lower lip. "She wouldn't come quietly."

The warden shoved her to Rock, who checked out her split lip. "I'm sorry about that." His hand rose slowly. She flinched as it moved toward her, but he only gently brushed the hair from her face. "We need the password to re-program the flight plan."

"Commander?"

Ryker did not turn around. "Do as he says."

"Where are we going, Commander?"

Rock watched the exchange between them. She purposefully ignored him, showing that she still believed in her commander and that somehow, maybe, he had a plan to escape this nightmare she had awoken to. He would allow her to think that for as long as it served his purpose of getting this ship turned around and back on course. But it was starting to grind on his nerves. He was number one, not Ryker.

"We're going home."

"What about the prisoners?"

Rock stepped in front of her. Rage boiled in his veins. His words came out strained, as he fought to control his pounding heartbeat and speeding pulse. "Will you please just enter the damn password?"

"No."

The word knocked him back a step. He had not expected that. His hand itched. The mouth opened, but he couldn't risk converting her yet. If she died, they had no way of turning the ship around.

"Commander, do you have the password stored somewhere in the memory banks?"

Ryker's face went blank and he stared at the floor. A moment later, he looked up and shook his head. "All I could dig up were protocols. I would need to announce an emergency and contact Earth. We won't be allowed to land on any of the seven human-zoned planets."

"We don't want that." He turned his attention back to Demi. "Enter the password."

"No."

He wanted to kill her. Not convert her—*kill* her. Deader than the five points of the starfish he arrived on. "Commander Ryker, contact Earth. Tell them about a riot in the cells and that prisoners were on the loose. Navigational Officer Demi Lang was killed in a sexual confrontation. Assign a new navigational officer."

"Yes, sir."

"No." Demi tapped the screen. "Done."

Commander Ryker confirmed deactivation. Rock was pleased. He still wanted to kill Demi but held off on that impulse. She could wait. "Turn us around," he ordered.

She did as ordered.

Rock stared out into space as the large ship slowly turned 180 degrees. The stars he wanted to see finally came into view. He was pleased. All defenses he knew about were taken care of. No auto switch and hopefully all the bombs were being disengaged. Better safe than sorry. He had learned from his last failure. It would not happen again.

Ryker said, "Home, here we come."

"There is still work to be done." Rock approached the chair. "There is a girl on board, yes?"

"Yeah, somewhere. Demi knows."

"Take me to her."

Demi nodded reluctantly.

Rock smiled. "Good. Ryker, go to the warden's office. We will set up base there for the coming hours."

"Okay, everyone," Ryker said, standing up, "follow me." He walked off the Bridge as all the crew members formed a line to follow.

"Not you, Demi," Rock said. "We need to get that girl."

DEMI WATCHED ROCK APPROACH. She knew him, but his actions confused her. He seemed intent on getting back to Earth and all the crew was somehow under his command. Didn't he realize that, once he got home, he would be arrested again and this time he would get the Cryo-Death—the worst punishment to known? Frozen forever, the brain was kept active with electricity pulsing through it, so the prisoner knew what was happening and slowly went insane. The torment was never-ending.

Standing next to her, Rock struck an imposing figure. The man looked chiseled from granite. He resembled a Greek god she had seen several years back on an old twenty-first-century holo-disk. But he stank.

"Shower much?" she asked.

"I was finishing a routine when this happened."

"When what happened?"

Rock smiled. "You may never know."

The last of the crew boarded the elevator on its second trip.

"Take me to the girl. I believe there is a boy on board as well."

Demi nodded.

"What is he?"

"Her younger brother."

Rock seemed to consider her answer. His eyes narrowed, then he smiled. "Remarkable. The same two children from the last attempt." He shook his head slowly as he headed to the elevator. He looked at Demi. "Some things are destined, aren't they?"

Demi didn't answer.

"Wouldn't you say?" he asked.

"I have no idea what you're talking about."

They entered the elevator. "What floor?" he asked.

"Sixth."

"Very well." As the doors closed, he said, "We latched onto a ship in dead space and sensed something special when the girl entered the room. We opened a crack and allowed the distress signal to get out. And here we are." He smiled to himself. "And to think we were just looking for food." A small laugh escaped.

"Destiny," Demi said.

"Indeed. This time it is meant to be."

The elevator opened on level six.

Demi led him down the corridor. "We put them in empty quarters."

Looking around, Rock said, "My men have not reached this sector yet."

"They won't find many people here. We're running a skeleton crew on this trip."

They walked past a room. "Wait." Rock looked at the door. "Open it."

Demi complied. She waved her hand under the scanner. The door opened. "Illumination," she said, and the gloomy room filled with light. The room was barren—no furniture, no whiteware, no kids.

"All right, let's go."

Demi shrugged and led the way out. The door closed automatically behind her. "Most of these rooms are empty."

"Take me directly to the kids."

"They're just down here. This way." She hoped her voice sounded dull and lifeless. Demi planned to trap him in one of the rooms. He wouldn't be able to leave; his DNA print would read as prisoner and an alert would go to Earth.

"They're in this room," she said, reaching the end of the corridor.

"Why put them way back here?"

Demi thought fast. She needed a reason he would believe. "They are under quarantine and this is the best we could do."

"Are they the only people on this floor?"

"No. There are some crew members, but they are with Commander Ryker."

Rock looked satisfied with this answer. He pushed her forward. "Take me to them."

Demi waved her hand and the door opened, revealing a pitch-black interior. She stepped to the side as Rock pushed past her and entered the dark room.

"Illumination," he said.

No change.

He turned to Demi. "Are you sure—"

She waved her hand past the panel and the door swooshed shut. A loud sigh escaped and she smiled at the shut door. Then the smile wavered. No shouts or threats came from inside. She took an involuntary step back from the door. Rock should be going crazy behind it, pounding it like an enraged animal.

She turned and ran down the corridor, headed for the kids' quarters. Reaching a T-junction, she stopped and reconsidered her intentions. No one knew where the kids were. It was best to keep them there—unaware and safe.

She needed a place to think and formulate a plan. But how long did she have? Accessing a wall panel, she noted a digital clock displayed 4:30. With Rock locked away, his followers wouldn't know what to do. A few might get suspicious when he didn't show.

Time. Demi still had time.

The Bridge—the main control center of the ship—was deserted. She could turn on the auto-destruct system again and radio for help. She took off at a fast pace, but not running. Old training memories started to surface—stuff she hadn't thought about for years. From the main control, she could shut down all elevators and kill all communications within the ship. She quickened her step, turning the walk into a jog.

LAURA AWOKE WITH A start, unaware that she'd fallen asleep. She hoped Commander Ryker hadn't shown up. Her night clothes were drenched with sweat. She sat up in bed and found Jared playing the immersion zombie game. She frowned but decided to let him have his fun. Sweat rolled down her cheek, tickling her. She wiped it off with the back of her hand and got out of bed. She looked at the illuminated wall clock. A quarter to five. It should be illegal waking this early.

She walked to a pile of clothes she had ordered before going to bed. Her stack was tidy and in organized manner. She glanced at her brother and saw his pile scattered all over the place. Her brother had made this place home for now. She'd also started to relax here. It had just been her and Jared for so long that it felt weird to have others to talk with. Her thoughts brought Ensign Coffey to mind. *Mainly him*, she thought.

"I'm going to take a shower," she said to Jared, and then remembered nothing existed for him with immersion. Even if he turned around, he would not see her. The game world was 360 degrees, up and down, smells and all—bar taste and death. His mind was tricked into believing the game world until the character died and it all ended. Then the immersion field dropped.

Laura scooped up some clothes. Remembering Coffey was coming for breakfast, she decided on a black mini-skirt and a white top. She unwrapped the packages and placed the items neatly next to the bed. Heading to the shower, she made a U-turn and carefully placed the plastic in the bio-degrader unit.

In the shower, she activated the water button. With the water instantly hot, she stepped in and relished the flow streaming down her body and through her hair.

Drying herself, she heard the door announce a visitor. She froze. The door announcement chimed a second time. *Maybe it's*

Commander Ryker, she thought. *Or Ensign Coffey*. That thought brought a smile to her face.

Wrapping the towel tight around her body, she went to the viewer.

A clean-shaven young man's face appeared on the screen. "Hello there." He held a guard badge up to the screen. "We're searching for a prisoner named Rock." He removed his credentials. "We've been ordered by Commander Ryker to do a room-by-room search of all quarters and storage areas."

"This is the first I've heard of it."

A guilty look came over the man's face and he bit his bottom lip. "Yeah, we are, ah, trying to keep this on a low key."

"There's no one here except my brother and me."

"We need to enter, ma'am. For everyone's safety."

Laura hesitated. Something felt off about this whole situation. But he had ID and seemed sincere enough. And she had been asleep for hours. "Okay." The lack of human interaction, even for such a short time, made her wary of her ability to judge others. Waving her hand under the light panel, she smiled as the door opened.

Three men barged their way in. One grabbed her around the waist and lifted her easily into a fireman's carry.

She struggled against him. "Let me go," she yelled, punching his back.

From her viewpoint, she couldn't see what the other men were doing, but she could hear them searching, opening doors and closets, and whatnot.

"All clear," one of them said. "Stupid kid over there is in an immersion game."

"Good." The man holding her dumped her on the bed. He paused, staring at her.

She looked down to see what had grabbed his attention and noticed her towel had opened across one thigh. She quickly pulled it shut.

"Don't do that, lovely."

The guard approached her. He held up his hand, exposing the mouth in the palm.

Laura slid off the bed and jumped to her feet. The guard grabbed her shoulder and his teeth sank in.

ROCK LOOKED AROUND. Another barren room. That woman, the navigator, had tricked him well. The thought of being double-crossed never entered his mind and he was angry at himself for playing into her hands. His previous role had always been one of nightmares. Infect the children of Earth with dreams that terrify. The strong ones would pass along the nightmares unaware of their actions. Not knowing they were building an army for his high priest. Now he had the honor of bringing Zathuphu back.

Stuck in this room, he felt helpless. He still needed three more for the ceremony and time was growing short. The door wouldn't open and he failed to break it down. And he had not remembered to bring a communicator with him.

The room jolted—not physically, just in his vision.

Something had happened.

Just now.

He felt something deep down and he searched his being for it. And found it.

The girl, the carrier of Zathuphu. He could taste her blood in his mouth as a vision of her waved into his mind. He could not allow them to damage her. He had to get out of here.

Think, damn you, think!

Feeding. Who had he fed off when he got free, apart from Rock? Which DNA would not be recognized as a prisoner? Whose blood had mixed with his?

The warden.

Perfect.

Rock held his hand up and bit into the mouth hole, ripping the skin, and cutting the flesh. He smeared the blood over his other hand, coating it well. Satisfied he had done a good job, he hurried to the scanner and waved his hand under it.

The door slid open.

He rushed down the hall, trying to sense the girl. With her taste on his tongue, he was able to track the direction by the strength of the blood. He looked up, staring at the ceiling. That woman had led him one floor lower.

Urgency was paramount now.

ENSIGN COFFEY FOUGHT off a hundred intruders. Only his team remained alive and active. Everyone looked at him for commands. Communications were down and no help seemed forthcoming in the immediate future. Destroyed bodies lay around him and on the battlefield—limbs missing, vests coated with blood, and a few survivors screaming for help.

The enemy used an outdated chess defense; half the force was lost before this information came to light. They used the Dragon Variation of the Sicilian Defense. Coffey knew nothing of the game of chess and was at a disadvantage right away. Before communications dropped, HQ had their best and brightest scouring the archives for breaching strategies to win this battle. He also had no idea what started this war. It cost a lot of lives since the drones proved useless in this environment.

And now he was the highest-ranking soldier on the field.

Laser blasts and sonic bombs stopped for a moment.

From his rear pocket, he removed the tablet and accessed the map. He expanded it to 3D, with three hundred- and sixty-degree views, and studied the image from several viewpoints.

Three booms sounded close. Ensign Coffey instinctively dived to the blood-soaked ground. No explosions came. Silence filled the battlefield.

Three more booms rocked the silence and Coffey realized someone had banged on his door.

His eyes snapped open. His sheets were damp with sweat and had twisted around his legs.

Kicking free, he got up and headed to the door, rubbing sleep from his eyes. The dream lingered with him just moments before it dissipated. At the door, he activated the viewer but saw no one.

Must have been the dream, he thought.

Someone screamed. It sounded like Barbs next door. Ensign Coffey opened his door enough to see two men push through into her room.

Ensign Coffey closed the door quickly and silently.

Hanging on a hook next to his uniform was his phaser. Pulling it from his holster, he considered contacting Commander Ryker, but decided against it, feeling haste was more important.

Heart racing, he entered the corridor. Barbs' door swung open. From inside he heard a muffled scream, then silence. He sidled up to the door jamb and peeked around the corner. One of the men had his hand over Barbs' mouth.

Coffey entered, phaser aimed. "Let her go."

The two men turned. As the hand came away from her face, Coffey saw a snakelike creature scurry up her nose. Barbs dropped in a heap.

"What in the name..." He fired. The phaser blast struck the second man, knocking him to the ground. The hand guy raised his hand to show the mouth with pointed teeth.

A phaser blast knocked him back a step. He advanced, mumbling words Coffey didn't understand. A second blast didn't affect the man.

Turning the charge from stun to kill, Coffey took careful aim and fired the third blast at the mouth.

Screaming, the man dropped to his knees. Blood oozed from his eyes and nose. A black creature dropped from his nose and wriggled across the floor.

"Help me," the man whispered before collapsing.

The snakelike thing lay still.

At the man's side, he said, "What's going on? What is that?"

"It's the Slithereen." His voice was barely a whisper. Suddenly his eyes opened wide.

Coffey spun around, dropping onto his back, and fired a kill shot at Barbs' raised hand. She fell to her knees. The Slithereen scurried toward Coffey. A kill blast set it on fire. Behind her, the other man slowly stood up. In his palm, a deformed mouth fashioned. It twisted oblong and not into a perfect circle like the other two.

Coffey sensed a shot to the mouth was not necessary this time and aimed a killing blast at the man's head. The shot punched him into the air and he crashed down hard. A Slithereen slid from his nose and died on his cheek.

Barbs moaned. She shook her head and slowly tried to stand. Coffey noticed and, quick to react, offered assistance, which she declined. Back on her feet, she stumbled to her bed and dropped onto the mattress. She sighed loudly.

Swallowing a lump in his throat, Coffey left the room. He had known Barbs for years and hearing her death sigh saddened him more than he thought it would.

Back in his room, he quickly dressed. *If these men were here, were others roaming the ship?* A terrifying thought entered his head. *Were Laura and Jared, okay?*

He exited his room at a run, phaser in his hand and at the ready.

PAIN SCREAMED THROUGH her shoulder. It felt like a hundred tiny teeth were gnawing on her, trying to chew off a slab of meat. She wanted to scream but the agony stole her voice, strangling her vocal cords into silence.

The guard took his hand away from Laura's shoulder. His expression appeared pained, in turn, etching confusion into his face.

Laura saw her chance to move back a step as the guard stared at his palm. She stole furtive glances here and there, noting the location of the men and hoping for a way out of this before it escalated into her worst nightmare.

Looking at her, the guard said, "What are you?"

Trying her best to keep her voice steady, she said, "I'm no one. A nobody."

The big guy stepped past the guard and drove a forceful backhand strike across her face, knocking Laura against the bed. A warm trickle of blood fell from her nose.

Squatting to be at eye-level with the girl, the guard said, "It's just better this way."

"What's better?"

"Everything."

The big guy pushed his hand down. "I don't know about you, Patterson, but me and Tommy been locked up a long while. We wouldn't mind a bit-a fun with the girl before you bring her to our way of thinking."

Laura pushed off the side. Seeing her chance to run, she bolted for the door.

Tommy moved fast and cut her off ten feet from the door. His vice-like grip wrapped around her throat and he effortlessly pushed her back to the bed. Heart racing, she fought against his grip to no avail. His hand didn't move.

The big guy pounced on her. His weight crushed her into the mattress. She tried to block out what was happening but the man's meaty paws yanked on the towel.

Panic mode set in.

Laura's hands pummeled his chest and head, her legs kicked out and she screamed. Her fingers clawed at his hair and pulled hard.

"Get her hands off me!" Tommy's fist smashed down on her mouth.

Pain exploded from the split lip but she refused to submit.

The towel was pulled to the side and she realized her first time would be this way.

Tommy forced her arms across her chest and pinned them there.

The big guy leaned forward. Against her ear, he whispered, "You're gonna enjoy this."

She turned her head to the side.

"This is how a real man—"

Shouts erupted. The big man flew off her and her arms were released. She quickly scrambled to the head of the bed and saw Coffey, arms swinging and legs snapping. The big guy couldn't move with his trousers around his knees. A kick to his groin dropped him—a knee to the head finished him. Patterson lay unconscious near the bed. She watched Tommy do some sort of Kata, but Coffey stepped in and drove his fist into the other's throat. He grabbed the head and snapped it a full one-eighty. Tommy's limp body hit the floor next to Jared, who was so completely immersed in his zombie game, he noticed nothing.

The big guy groaned. Coffey moved with speed. He leaped in the air and crashed down. Laura heard breaking bones. She leaned to the side of the bed and saw the big guy's face partially collapsed.

Coffey turned to face her. He quickly turned away.

Laura looked down at herself. The towel was open but bunched around her hips. She stepped into her skirt and pulled on her shirt. "Thank you," she said softly.

"I'm just glad you're okay."

Off the bed, she embraced him. "Thank you, thank you."

"Don't cry," he said, pulling her off him.

Her tear-filled eyes stared up at him.

"It's not over yet."

Using the back of her hand, Laura wiped her eyes and took a deep breath to calm down. Coffey inspected one of the prison guards.

"What's going on?"

"I don't know," Coffey said after inspecting Patterson. "All comm links are blocked."

Laura ran her hand through her hair. She couldn't help but think a similar thing had happened on the other ship, although she had never been as close to the terror as moments ago.

"Unhook your brother. We gotta get moving."

"Where are we going?"

"There's only one place to go. The Bridge."

"Wait." Laura disappeared into the bathroom.

"We don't have time for this." A hint of panic vibrated his voice.

Laura exited a moment later with a med-kit pressed to her lip. "I can't let him see me injured. He'd freak out, and we don't need that." She exposed her shoulder. "Is it covered?"

Ensign Coffey nodded.

JARED, STILL AFFECTED by the immersion game, unsteadily made his way along the corridor. The floor did not seem straight, nor did it seem level. His sight waved in and out of focus, and several times he thought he saw zombies coming around corners or through the walls.

He did not share this information with Laura or what's-his-name, as he knew he would be forced to listen to a lecture about the after-effects of immersion games and why they were illegal.

His sister was several steps ahead of him and moving fast. Jared struggled to keep up and at times fell behind, like now.

Laura turned to him. "Hurry," she whispered harshly.

He didn't reply but wondered why the big rush.

From the corner of his eye, he spotted a skin-rotted zombie lumbering towards him. His heart skipped a beat. *It's not real.* He had to remember that. *I am not plugged in...am I?*

Up ahead, he saw the lift that would take them directly to the Bridge. "Why are we going there?"

Laura and what's-his-name didn't answer.

What's-his-name pressed the lift UP button and waited.

The doors opened.

They rode up in silence. Something was wrong; Jared could feel it hanging in the air. He had heard hushed words: *everything's going to be okay now* and *you're fine.* What he was talking about, Jared had no idea. But something must have happened while in the game. Laura's lip looked puffy. He saw a small cut, not that noticeable, but he knew she didn't have that at bedtime.

The lift doors opened and they came face to face with Demi holding a sonic blaster, and it was pointed at them.

ROCK CLIMBED THE METAL ladder to the next level. He didn't trust the lift registering his presence by some bio-scan he wasn't aware of. He climbed nimbly and fast. Holding onto the sides of the ladder, not the rungs, he scurried up.

At the next level, he used the emergency button to open the doors. Exiting the elevator shaft, he squatted down, one hand on the floor for added balance, and inhaled deeply.

The blood scent rose to greet him—a faint aroma tainted by the odor of other blood. All the scents pointed in the same direction. Rock was on his feet and running before he knew it.

He rounded a corner and came to an open door.

Stepping over the threshold, he saw Patterson struggling to get to his feet and two others dead. The Slithereen lay partly out of their nose. The smooth skin was dry and cracked.

The rest of the room appeared empty.

He approached Patterson and helped him into a sitting position, using the bed as a backrest. "What happened?"

Patterson shook his head as if to clear it. "Someone attacked us from behind."

"How is that possible? There were three of you."

Struggling to his feet, Patterson tried to find his balance.

"The girl is the vessel of the Great One."

Patterson's eyes widened. "We didn't know."

"How were you attacked?"

"Those two," he pointed at the dead bodies, "wanted some fun before turning her."

Blood boiled into Rock's face making his cheeks flame. "You bloody fool!" he raged, grabbing Patterson by the throat and lifting him off the floor. "What have you done?"

"She got a cut lip and a small bite, that's all. I swear."

Rock heard no fear in the man's voice. He told the truth. Releasing his hold, he let Patterson drop to the floor. He didn't rise immediately.

All this was Rock's fault and he knew that. He had given the order to convert everyone. There was no directive to not treat all children the same as others, and he had not mentioned anything to them about pleasures of the flesh. They had been prisoners for a long time, the Slithereen as well. He should have thought of this. But he hadn't. *What's done is done.*

He helped Patterson back to his feet. "Where have they gone?"

"I do not know. But an ensign is the one who helped them."

"And an ensign would look for his commander."

Patterson smiled. "And the commander is usually on the bridge."

THOMAS RYKER WOKE UP. It was more like awareness blooming, understanding slowly making its way into his conscious mind, than waking. His consciousness inhabited by another being...a...Slithereen. He was suddenly aware of everything happening aboard his ship. And the plan they had.

In his mind, he heard a series of screeches with pauses here and there. He understood this to be language. And he understood it, like a child understands its native language.

You die, it said.

Ryker didn't know how to answer.

Why you no die?

"It's hard to kill me," he said. He didn't feel his mouth moving or hear his words.

You die now.

"Try it."

Raging hot pain burned against his conscious mind. The pain crippled him. He had no voice with which to scream, but that did not stop him. Mixed with the scream, he heard the Slithereen laughing.

It spoke in another language to him; one that he could not comprehend.

But he understood evil and he fought against it.

He turned the scream into laughter. And the pain abated.

The Slithereen retaliated.

Commander Ryker moved his hands to his face and scratched at the nose.

Stop it.

"Like hell, I will stop." Thomas dug his fingers into his nose. "You lose."

Pain worse than before slammed his consciousness. Ryker felt himself fading. He felt his arms fall to his sides.

Ryker stopped.

You lose.

Ryker remained silent.

Finally, you die.

Silence.

Ryker hid himself in the cloud that covered his consciousness.

And waited...

AS COMMANDED, EVERYONE waited in the warden's office. The entire crew was on the Bridge at the time of arrival. The room, not small by any means, was crowded and apparently the new HQ of this operation for bringing Zathuphu back to Earth. Standing around the room, no one spoke. They all waited. The warden noticed Ryker insert his fingers into his nose and scratch around. He almost said something until the man's hand dropped to his sides.

Noticing a line of red dribble over his top lip, Warden Johnson asked, "Are you all right?"

"All is as it should be."

"Your nose is bleeding."

"It is of little concern."

Warden Johnson nodded. He sat in his seat behind the big desk and twiddled his fingers. He sighed loudly.

The warden turned on the monitors of the cells. A large holo-screen appeared. The cells were a mess of blood and gore. Some inmates hadn't taken to the Slithereen as well as others. He felt sorry for them; they weren't destined to witness the return of the great priest and the Old Ones. The time fast approached. He could feel it in the air.

"It's amazing," he said to Ryker, who gave him a quizzical look. "It's amazing that a primitive race of humans could banish him and the Old Ones."

"Read the memory banks."

Warden Johnson closed his eyes. In the darkness, he saw the beautiful Zathuphu and the humans wearing animal skins. They quaked in this presence. As they should. Flashes lit the sky, quick explosions of brilliance. Darkness followed.

"They had help," Ryker said.

No further images showed to Warden Johnson. His eyes snapped open when he heard Zathuphu's wail. It agonized and pained him to hear these sounds. "It's best not to remember," he said, tears welling in his eyes.

Ryker nodded. "Then don't."

Changing the subject, the warden said, "We should have heard from Rock by now. It's been too long. He said he would meet us here."

"And he will. Patience has served us for a millennium. It will serve us a few minutes longer."

Warden Johnson panned the camera. He saw a few prisoners sitting on the floor, staring into space. Using the intercom, he ordered, "Stand up."

No reaction.

"I said, 'stand up.'"

Nothing.

"Braindead," he mumbled to himself. Humans are so weak. How did they become top of the food chain? Outside help again? He doubted it. His information on the human race showed a history of weapon creation and increasing aggression, not just to food sources, but to their fellow man. Nothing had changed. Zathuphu would put a stop to that. With his legion of Outer Gods ruled by *Azathoth* and *Shub-Niggurath*, the Black Goat, and the intermediary *Nyarlathotep*, humans would once again quake in his presence for time eternal.

Ryker activated his comm. He tried to radio Rock but got only static.

"Try me," the warden said.

Ryker did. Static was the reply.

"Someone's on the Bridge and they have disabled communications."

Ryker nodded.

"What should we do?"

Commander Ryker seemed to consider the options. "We give Rock five minutes and then we head up to the Bridge."

ENSIGN COFFEY'S HANDS shot straight up. "Whoa. Don't shoot."

The sonic blaster did not lower.

Jared pushed past Laura. "What's going on?" he asked, looking Demi in the eyes. "These two are talking about something they don't want me to know."

"I was attacked," Laura blurted out. "Three men came into my room. Two wanted to hurt me and the other said something about a conversion. Coffey helped me."

Demi looked at Coffey.

"I didn't open my door," he said. "By the time I woke up, they had moved on to Barbs' room. Something is really messed up here. First point of contact is the Bridge. My comm is not working." He shrugged. "And here we are."

"Are you hurt, Laura?" Jared asked.

"No. I'm fine, thanks to Ensign Coffey."

Demi lowered the sonic blaster. "Sorry," she said. "Long story short, there is a foreign life form on board and it's not friendly. It has the entire crew."

"Did you—" Coffey motioned to the auto-destruct activator, "—push it?"

She shook her head. "The code's changed."

"Manual activation?"

"Guarded."

Jared said, "What are you talking about?"

"Nothing to worry about, little man."

He decided he didn't like what's-his-name any longer. "I'm thirteen."

Ensign Coffey went to the comms panel. "We need to contact Earth."

"I de-activated it."

"Why?"

"To stop the others from communicating."

Coffey ran his hands through his short hair.

The lift lowered.

"Damn it," Demi shouted. "Forgot to lock it." She dashed to another panel and punched codes one after the other. "Done."

Jared felt the tension in the room and he joined his sister against the far wall, staying out of the way. He grabbed his sister's hand. "It's like last time," he said.

Demi stopped and spun to face him. "What did you say?"

"We didn't have a chance to tell Commander Ryker," Laura said. "There was something onboard the other ship. We escaped before it exploded."

"Clarify 'something onboard.'"

"A creature," Jared said, remembering the beast withering in the corridor.

Demi sighed. "This is no time for games, damn it, Jared."

"No games," Laura said. "An alien being of unknown origin attacked our transport ship and breached the outer hull, eventually making its way through and destroying everyone and everything."

The lift opened.

"I lost an outer god on that day." Rock smiled. "Live and learn, right?" He held up his right hand. Blood dribbled down his wrist. "The warden's blood. DNA overrides all lockdowns."

Demi raised the sonic blaster.

"Seriously?"

"Try me. Get your hands up."

"You're willing to risk the ship?"

"Shoot him," Jared yelled. He didn't know this man, had never seen his face before, but something about the guy sent daggers of fear into his heart. "Kill him, Demi."

"She won't, boy. One shot and this room vanishes in an instant, as will half the lower decks." He smiled. "That's a lot of lives."

"Kill him." Jared pleaded, his eyes starting to water.

"Those people are dead now anyway."

Rock snorted. "Only the soul is dead. The Slithereen controls its host, that is all. They are not zombies."

At the word zombies, Jared's tears dried up. In his mind, he saw rusted barrels scattered about the bridge, a blue sky replaced the ceiling, fields of grass loomed before him, blades swayed in the gentle breeze, and somewhere far off someone groaned, "Brrraaaiiinnnzzzhhh."

The lift started down, the sound startling all but Rock. "I see you look confused, Demi. You forgot high-ranking DNA prints." His voice turned soft and encouraging. "You're in a panic, my dear. Simple, basic protocols have been forgotten." He took a step toward her. "Why don't you hand me that sonic blaster and our way to a better—safer—outcome?" Gently, ever so gently, he pulled it from her grasp.

Demi exhaled as if she had been hit.

"Silly bitch." Rock drove the butt of the blaster into the side of her head, dropping her unconscious to the floor.

Ensign Coffey had his phaser pointed at Rock.

Something bashed into the ship.

Laura screamed.

Coffey lost balance.

Jared searched for zombies.

Rock laughed.

Internal alarms filled the Bridge.

"Collision, collision, collision," repeated over and over again, joined by the loud whir sound.

DEMI STIRRED ON THE floor. A hardwired need for survival and the alarms sounding on the Bridge roused her. She saw Rock step past her as another collision sent off a number of alarms. Mustering all the strength she could, she climbed onto her knees first, then, using the panel, pulled herself to her feet. With blurred sight, she tried to make out the flashing light pads. Finding the one she needed from memory more than sight, Demi slapped her palm on it as a blue light filled the Bridge.

From the corner of her eye, she saw Laura rise off the floor. Her arms were raised at her sides and her head fell back. A pinpoint of red shot through the blue and slammed into the teen's chest.

"No. No. No. No. No," Rock screamed. "She's not for you, Cxaxukluth."

A deep booming voice filled the Bridge. "My father Azathoth is dead because of your failure, Slithereen."

Rock's face turned a deep red.

"I take what is yours."

"She's not mine. She is for Zathuphu."

Demi slapped the light pad again, this time she left her hand on the panel as it authorized her DNA print.

"Shields up."

The blue light vanished. The red beam of light vanished. And Laura fell to the floor.

Rock was at her side instantly. He gently slapped her face. "Hey, girl, wake up. Are you all right?"

Her eyes snapped open. A pulsing red light emanated from them.

A BLUE LIGHT FILLED the room.

"Is that him?" the warden asked.

"I doubt it," Commander Ryker said. "Seven of us are needed for the ceremony." He looked at everyone in the room. The others were turning their hands in the light as if they were trying to feel it, the warden also joined in.

He, on the other hand, felt anger, but he did not know why. The Slithereen was an ancient branch of The Elder Gods; they were harsh but fair in judgment, whereas The Outer Gods were little more than violent, deformed creatures.

Had an Outer God somehow broken through the 'Centre Universe'? Not a thought he wanted to dwell on. The consequences would be horrific. Not just for the Slithereen but for the universe, as the resulting war would be all-encompassing. The universe could cease to be.

The blue light suddenly vanished. His anger vanished. "Something's wrong." Commander Ryker felt it in his gut.

"What?" the warden asked.

"Not sure, but we have to find Rock. Now!" Ryker pushed past the female crew and opened the door. He turned to the warden. "Now, I said."

Warden Johnson moved from behind his desk. "Rock said to stay here."

"And I say, let's go." He stepped out the door.

"You're not the real commander, you know."

Ryker ignored him and headed to the lift, knowing he would follow.

ROCK STUMBLED AWAY from the girl as she slowly rose to her feet. In a voice, not hers, she said, "Zathuphu is dead. I feasted on his bones as he slept, waiting for the stars to align."

"You lie," Rock muttered, still backing away from her.

"Laura?" Ensign Coffey said, also taking a step back.

The body of Laura turned to face him. "She is here, but not for long."

"I don't understand what's going on."

Laura laughed. Her arms rose to chest height, palms up. "The first humans didn't understand either. We nearly wiped you all out. This time we will not fail."

Demi saw Rock raise the sonic blaster. She hoped the blast would not destroy the ship, but she was willing to die if it meant saving Earth from these creatures. The thing inside Laura started to lose interest in Coffey. She had to keep it occupied to give Rock time for a clean shot. "You failed the last time, what makes you think you will win this time? Nothing's changed. We will fight you with everything we have."

Laura faced her. "Go'thax is dead."

"Who?"

"The child—half man, half god. The so-called 'Missing Link.'" In her palms, two balls of energy formed, spinning in a tight circle and gathering speed.

"One of yours—"

"He's nothing! A foot soldier. A weak excuse for existence. I am not." In her palms, the balls swelled to the size of both her hands.

"Cxaxukluth, why do you hate your brother so much?" Rock asked in a soft voice.

"He is not my brother! HE'S A DEFORMITY." Laura spun around to face Rock, the balls of energy blended into one and expanded. "HE IS WEAK! I AM NOT!" The ball spun in the air between her palms and turned a dark red with wisps of bright yellow shooting across the surface. "Earth is—"

Rock fired.

The sonic blast hit the red ball absorbing all energy—

"No," Laura muttered.

The red ball turned white and slammed into her chest, taking her off her feet. Laura flipped twice and crashed down on the control panel, and slid unconscious to the floor.

Jared screamed and ran to his sister. Rock reached her first and pushed him aside. "Wait, boy," he said, keeping the sonic blaster aimed at the unmoving body. Using his foot, he rolled her face up.

Demi dropped next to Laura and brushed her hair from her face.

The elevator doors opened and Commander Ryker entered, followed by Warden Johnson.

Rock looked at them. "Cxaxukluth was here." He pointed at the girl by his feet.

Laura groaned and rolled onto her side. In her voice, she said, "The family knows." She again dropped onto her back. "Yog-Sothoth comes."

Rock grabbed her in a headlock and easily lifted her off the floor. "Quickly," he ordered. "To the airlock, before Cxaxukluth transforms into his true form." He started dragging the limp body.

Demi heard Jared crying and her heart went out to him, but she also agreed with Rock. That beast could not be allowed to transform on board. She couldn't let these three Slithereen remain either, especially with the ship on course to Earth. She didn't know what to do. Ensign Coffee leaned against a control panel. He looked to be in shock, staring forward, focused on nothing. She noticed his eyes were glazed.

To Rock, she said, "Could someone pick up her legs so she doesn't have to be dragged like that? It'll make the trip to the airlock faster."

Rock nodded. "Warden, grab her legs."

Commander Ryker stared at Jared.

Demi quickly moved to the boy's side and held him close. "Get away from him," she hissed. Ryker didn't respond. His face creased in deep concentration. She drew the boy closer, determined to keep him as safe as possible.

"Ryker," Rock said. "Need you to open the doors."

No response.

Rock placed Laura on the floor and raised his sonic blaster.

"No," Demi cried out, "there's no counter energy source. You'll blow the ship apart."

Ryker shook his head and turned to Rock. "Internal battle. He's gone now."

Rock lowered the blaster. "Open the damn doors."

Commander Ryker looked at Demi and winked, then opened the elevator doors.

"I'm coming," Jared said. "I must see."

Demi held him firmly locked into her arms, though she didn't think it was the right thing to do. Maybe Jared hoped Laura would suddenly return to her old self. Wishful thinking, but she couldn't refuse him and released her grip. He got to his feet fast and stopped the elevator doors from closing.

"Boy, you should stay here."

"No, Rock. I wanna see you do this to my sister. Then I can kill you."

Rock laughed. "I like your attitude. Then let's make this a party."

Demi stepped into the elevator as the doors shut. She planned on keeping a close eye on both Rock and Jared and intervene if the kid tried something stupid.

JARED KEPT HIS EYES on his sister. Rock and the warden watched the numbers drop as the lift took them down to the storage dock where rubbish and human waste got jettisoned towards the nearest sun.

Jared got out of the lift first and ran to the airlock. He opened the doors and turned to face Demi. She stood at the side, her eyes locked on his as Rock and the warden carried Laura past her. The commander followed. He didn't look at her as he passed.

All three entered the airlock.

"You have to place her close to the door," Jared said.

Demi watched Jared carefully.

Commander Ryker turned to Demi. "Close the door," he said.

Jared closed the door.

"What are you doing?" Rock dropped Laura and dashed to the control panel. It didn't react to his DNA reading.

Commander Ryker opened his hand, exposing a dead Slithereen. He let it fall to the floor.

Rock's fists were on him in an instant. Each strike a powerful blow, knocking the commander back as the warden also joined in the fight, tackling the commander to the floor.

"Open the door, you fool!" Rock yelled.

Warden Johnson quickly got to his feet.

Demi punched in the code to seal the doors.

The warden punched in his security code, but it didn't work. Demi pointed behind him. On a screen read-out was the words: *Hazardous Organisms detected. Expelling in…5…4…*

"No, please," the warden said.

…3…

Rock got up. He looked at Demi and said, "Slithereen can live in space."

…2…

Jared cupped his eyes against the glass.

…1…

A white gas filled the room. Rock and the warden started banging against the glass. Behind them, Demi saw Laura get to her knees and a look of confusion crossed her face. She started coughing instantly. With a heavy heart, Demi turned off the intercom.

"What's happening?" Jared asked.

"The gas kills all hazardous organisms. When Commander Ryker dropped the Slithereen, the computer detected the foreign substance."

The warden started coughing. A thin spray of blood splattered the glass. From his nose, the long black Slithereen dropped to the floor. It didn't move.

Rock stood defiant. He held his nose shut and seemed to be holding his breath.

Expelling gas.

Extractor fans activated, sucking out the white gas.

Organisms deceased.

Rock smiled.

Opening airlock.

"We'll meet again, Cxaxukluth."

The airlock doors opened and all four bodies were sucked out into space, along with the dead Slithereen.

Demi watched them drift away as the coldness of space coated their bodies in ice.

"She's gone." Jared placed his head against the glass and stared at the empty airlock.

Demi wrapped her arms around Jared. "The jobs not finished," she said softly. "There's many more Slithereen on board." She bent down to his height. "I want you to go to your room and lock the doors. And don't open them for anyone until we hit the Inspection Point. I'm sure the Crimes Unit will want to speak with you."

Jared nodded. A tear rolled down his cheek. "What are you going to do?"

"I'm going to help Ensign Coffey and we're going to do a floor-by-floor sweep."

IN HIS ROOM, JARED looked in the mirror. "Humans," he said. "Such fools."

Tentacles pushed free from his forearms. "Not yet," he whispered. "I must wait for Earth." He closed his eyes and took a deep, calming breath, enjoying the feeling as the appendages retracted into the human body.

He wondered why the Slithereen had thought he was Cxaxukluth. Did they not consider that more than one being could transport through the light?

Yog-Sothoth smiled.

Soon he would be on Earth, and there he would summon Zathuphu and the Elder Gods and reclaim what was once theirs.

END

BONUS SHORT STORY JUST FOR YOU.

Thanks for hanging around.

Constant Noise
Lee Pletzers ©2016

THE STREETS OF TOKYO teemed with people. A never-ending flow of suits and interesting fashion statements. Crowded sidewalks and jammed traffic. Bumper-to-bumper people and cars. Just another weekday in the land of the rising sun.

Unlike most ex-pats living here, it wasn't the culture that brought me, Jonathan Merced, from Perth. Old things and historic sites don't interest me. Never have.

I came here for the hi-tech gadgets and neon lights. After three years I can safely say, Japan is stuck in the past. There is one major intersection, on all the movies, that is 'bright lights, big city'; the rest is concrete, Pachinko, and the constant jabber of people on phones, to friends and to themselves. It never ends.

Only public transportation is silent, and I can get a chance to think. Riding the trains and buses is awesome. Totally quiet. It's the reason most people sleep on their way to work or home. I assume all the talking tires them out.

It doesn't tire me. I hate talking. It gets on my nerves. Angry, violent thoughts magically appear from nowhere, and in my vision, I'm stomping a person's head on the ground—harder and harder until it cracks open. If I'm especially exhausted, the vision turns darker, and sometimes other people come to the aid of the victim. In reality, they'd just get their phones out and stream to YouTube or some other site.

Way of the world, over here.

Jabber. Jabber. Jabber.

It's one of the few things that grate my nerves. I can handle a few minutes but ten to fifteen is pushing it. Even my MP3 player can't drown them out. They seem to get louder and louder. Before I know it someone has pissed me off, and in my head, they are getting stomped.

Such thoughts are not good but try as I might, I can't block them. The talking never stops on the streets, in offices, in hospitals, or riding elevators. The constant noise is maddening.

Today I have a late start at the school and that means I have to dodge talkers in the early afternoon. It's the worst time to be on the streets. The sun is out and the country is wide awake.

My ear buds are in and Megadeth is blaring, and for a short time all is right with the world. Until a woman next to me answers her phone. Her voice is high and shrill. Her laughter is the call of a hyena. She cackles and overreacts with every second breath. My Japanese is limited but I understand she is meeting this phone friend in five minutes. Five bloody minutes. She couldn't wait?

In my head, I picture grabbing her long wavy hair and yanking it backwards. Forcing her head to smack into the concrete and driving my boot down into her face—again and again and again. I imagine her screams dying out. Onlookers shocked but phones are uploading to YouTube. Live action attack. Foreigner goes nuts.

I imagine someone is calling the police on an old flip style phone. He can't upload video on that. The woman is unmoving on the ground. Her face is caved in. Calmly, I walk away, turned a corner and my mood changes. There's a happy feeling warming my insides. However, dark thoughts continue to ride with me, hanging around like a bad smell. They don't seem to want to vanish as they usually do.

There's a young man leaning against a convenience store wall and shouting on his phone. He's pissed at his mother. She found his magazines and DVDs, and he is disgusted she snooped through his things.

His jabbering is far too loud and he has no problem exposing himself as an asshole to the entire world. So many people openly stare at him.

I imagine in my bag is a kitchen knife. Full of confidence, I stride up to him. My right hand is inside my bag and it is gripping the knife handle. With a finger on my lips, I try to shush him. He should keep this call private.

He gives me a look of contempt and raises his volume.

Fine.

I'll shush him.

In my imagination, I move with lightning speed, my right hand comes out of my bag and the kitchen knife gets noticed too late. The man has no time to react. I drive the knife upward, under his chin, and into the roof of his mouth. The blade sticks in the mouth plate and I use my palm to punch it higher. His right eye deflates; goo sliding over the eyelid. I know that most of it is coating the knife's sharpened steel.

He drops his phone as he collapses to the ground. I can hear the mother on the other end still yelling at him. Her voice is as bad as his.

I imagine taking his wallet and learning his address. It's full of money, so I pocket the wallet for later.

His mother's voice follows me as I turn and cross the street. Onlookers are busy with phones while others have lost interest and continued on with their day.

I'm across the road in seconds and that damn woman's voice continues to grate my nerves. I can still hear the bitch. Her voice matches the shrill of police sirens filling the air.

Up ahead, I spot a black taxi. Its rear door is open, meaning it is looking for passengers.

Learning through the open back door, I ask if it's all right to get a lift. Sometimes they refuse foreign passengers. This cabbie says no problem and I show him the driver's license. He nods and pulls out into the traffic.

The ride is silent. Public transport is the best.

END

About the author

Award-winning author, Lee Pletzers is a displaced New Zealand writer of the weird, wonderful, and grotesque.

Since 2001, he has impacted the genre world, under the pen name Richard Lee. Over seventy short stories have slammed his name on anthologies and magazines across the globe; for example; The Literary Hatchet, Calamities Press, Under the Bed, and Nebula Rift. His short story "Water" was the finalist in the Sir Julius Vogel Awards NZ 2015 as was his horror fan site in 2010. Five novels affected humanity and two novellas were the icing on the cake.

He is now making the move into crime thrillers. He reads a lot of them and figures he might know a thing or two. His entrance into this genre starts with the Death World duology.

Buy me a coffee: https://www.buymeacoffee.com/leepletzers

Website: http://www.thriller.nz

Medium: https://medium.com/@threeand10

X (formally Twitter): https://www.twitter.com/threeand10

Instagram: https://www.instagram.com/threeand10/

Facebook: https://www.facebook.com/lpletzers/

YouTube: @whitenoise332

Books: https://books2read.com/ap/nOeB0x/Lee-Pletzers

Threads: @threeand10

Don't miss out!

Visit the website below and you can sign up to receive emails whenever Lee Pletzers publishes a new book. There's no charge and no obligation.

https://books2read.com/r/B-A-VUHC-ALNSB

BOOKS 2 READ

Connecting independent readers to independent writers.

Also by Lee Pletzers

Quincy's
The Thin You
The Last Watcher
The Armageddon Shadow
Chaos
The Last Church
Ellen
The Game
Rage
Water
No Rebound Weight Loss
How to Write a Book
Scorched Earth

Watch for more at www.thriller.nz.